D0578458

DATE DUE

NOV 2 2 2001		
JAN 0 3 2007		
FEB 2 2 2014		
MAY 0 9 2014		
JUL 1 6 2014		

E
Goode,   Goode, Diane
Diane   Mama's perfect
                    present

00.724
$14.95

Saguache County Public Library
Saguache, Colorado

Mama's Perfect Present

Diane Goode

PUFFIN BOOKS

Saguache County Public Library
Saguache, Colorado

PUFFIN BOOKS
Published by the Penguin Group
Penguin Putnam Books for Young Readers, 345 Hudson Street, New York, New York 10014, U.S.A.
Penguin Books Ltd, 27 Wrights Lane, London W8 5TZ, England
Penguin Books Australia Ltd, Ringwood, Victoria, Australia
Penguin Books Canada Ltd, 10 Alcorn Avenue, Toronto, Ontario, Canada M4V 3B2
Penguin Books (N.Z.) Ltd, 182-190 Wairau Road, Auckland 10, New Zealand

Penguin Books Ltd, Registered Offices: Harmondsworth, Middlesex, England

First published in the United States of America by Dutton Children's Books,
a division of Penguin Books USA Inc., 1996
Published by Puffin Books, a member of Penguin Putnam Books for Young Readers, 1999

1 3 5 7 9 10 8 6 4 2

children's Plus Ire. 6-13-00
00-724
$14.95

Copyright © Diane Goode, 1996
All rights reserved

THE LIBRARY OF CONGRESS HAS CATALOGED THE DUTTON EDITION AS FOLLOWS:
Goode, Diane.
Mama's perfect present / by Diane Goode. —
1st ed.   p.   cm.
Summary: Two children have some problems when they
take their dog along as they search for just the
right present for their mother's birthday.
ISBN 0-525-45493-4
[1. Birthdays—Fiction. 2. Gifts—Fiction. 3. Brothers and
sisters—Fiction. 4. Dogs—Fiction.] I. Title.
PZ7.G604Mam 1996 [E]—dc20 96-7776 CIP AC

Puffin Books ISBN 0-14-056549-3

Printed in the United States of America

Except in the United States of America, this book is sold subject to the condition that it
shall not, by way of trade or otherwise, be lent, re-sold, hired out, or otherwise circulated
without the publisher's prior consent in any form of binding or cover other than
that in which it is published and without a similar condition including
this condition being imposed on the subsequent purchaser.

For Peter

"Today is Mama's birthday. Hold on to Zaza's leash.
She can help us find the perfect present."

"Oh, la la! Look at the beautiful flowers.
Should we get Mama flowers?"

"Maybe not. Flowers are very pretty,
but they make some people's eyes water."

"How about a dress? This one is sensational,
and Mama loves red!"

"That dress was *too* sensational.
Mama doesn't like to show off."

"What sweet little songbirds.
Mama loves music."

"Those birds were very noisy.
They might disturb the neighbors."

"Do you think Mama would like
a special birthday cake?"

"A big cake would be hard to carry.
We might drop it on the way home."

"These shoes would look beautiful
on Mama. Shall I try them on?"

"Those shoes were not comfortable at all!
Mama could fall down in them."

"It's getting late, and we still haven't found
a present for Mama. What are we going to do?"

"Zaza! Wait for us!"

"I think this is just what we need.
I knew we would find something."

"Mama will be so surprised!"

"Happy birthday, Mama!"

"Thank you. It's perfect!"